MOTHERS ARE LIKE THAT

MOTHERS ARE LIKE THAT

by Carol Carrick
Illustrated by Paul Carrick

CLARION BOOKS
New York

Clarion Books
a Houghton Mifflin Company imprint
215 Park Avenue South, New York, NY 10003
Text copyright © 2000 by Carol Carrick
Illustrations copyright © 2000 by Paul Carrick
First Clarion paperback edition, 2006.

The illustrations were executed in acrylic paint.
The text was set in 26-point Galliard.
Book design by Carol Goldenberg.

www.clarionbooks.com

Printed in Singapore.

Library of Congress Cataloging-in-Publication Data
Carrick, Carol.
Mothers are like that / by Carol Carrick ; illustrated by Paul Carrick.
p.   cm.
Summary: A simple description of animal and human mothers caring for their young.
ISBN 0-395-88351-2
[1. Mother and child—Fiction. 2. Animals—Infancy—Fiction.]
I. Carrick, Paul, ill. II. Title.
PZ7.C2344 Mo 2000
[E]—dc21   99-16587
CIP

CL ISBN-13: 978-0-395-88351-8   CL ISBN-10: 0-395-88351-2
PA ISBN-13: 978-0-618-75241-6   PA ISBN-10: 0-618-75241-2

TWP 10 9 8 7 6 5

For you and me

—C.C. & P.C.

Mother cares for her babies
even before they're born.

Mothers are like that.

She has milk
for her hungry ones.

Mothers are like that.

Mother keeps her babies clean,

and close,

and safe from harm.

She can find them
in a crowd.

Mothers are like that.

When babies learn
to stand and walk,

Mother takes them out and shows them off.

Then they look
for treats

until it's time
to go home

to a soft bed,

a snuggle,

and a kiss good night.

Mothers are like that.